How Tzipi
the Bird
Got
Her Wings

D1416706

Also by Bernard M. Zlotowitz and Dina Maiben
Abraham's Great Discovery

Published in the United States by NightinGale Resources
Box 322
Cold Spring, New York 10516-0322

Library of Congress Catalog Card Number: 94-66712

ISBN 0-911389-05-9 (Hard cover)
ISBN 0-911389-06-7 (soft cover)

First Printing 1995
Printed in Hong Kong
Text is set in Korinna

To my beloved granddaughters, Andrea and Emma Zlotowitz, whose zest for life delights my life.

Bernard M. Zlotowitz

For Michael Aaron Nappa, who brings joy and delight.

Dina Maiben

To my sons Timour and Matthew Veksler.

Vitaliy Veksler

God made the heavens and the earth:
the sun, the moon and the stars
the mighty oceans and the dry land.

And God made the lions and tigers
the monkeys and donkeys
dogs and frogs
chipmunks and skunks
reptiles and crocodiles.

And God did not forget

snails and whales
butterflies and dragon flies
kangaroos and kinkajous.

God also made a beautiful garden filled with all kinds of trees and all sorts of bushes. There were grassy meadows, fields of berries and fruit trees of every kind. God covered the garden with a blanket of flowers, including tulips, daisies and roses. All around the garden flowed a stream of cool water.

All the animals lived in the garden. God said, "This is your garden to enjoy, but you must keep it neat and clean."

The animals loved this garden. All day there were trees to climb and flowers to smell, grass to roll in, sweet fruit to eat and cool water to drink.

When evening came, they were so tired that everyone went to bed without a grumble:

the lion and the lamb
the cat and the dog
the fox and the hare.

They all cuddled up together under the star-filled, moonlit sky, and none was afraid.

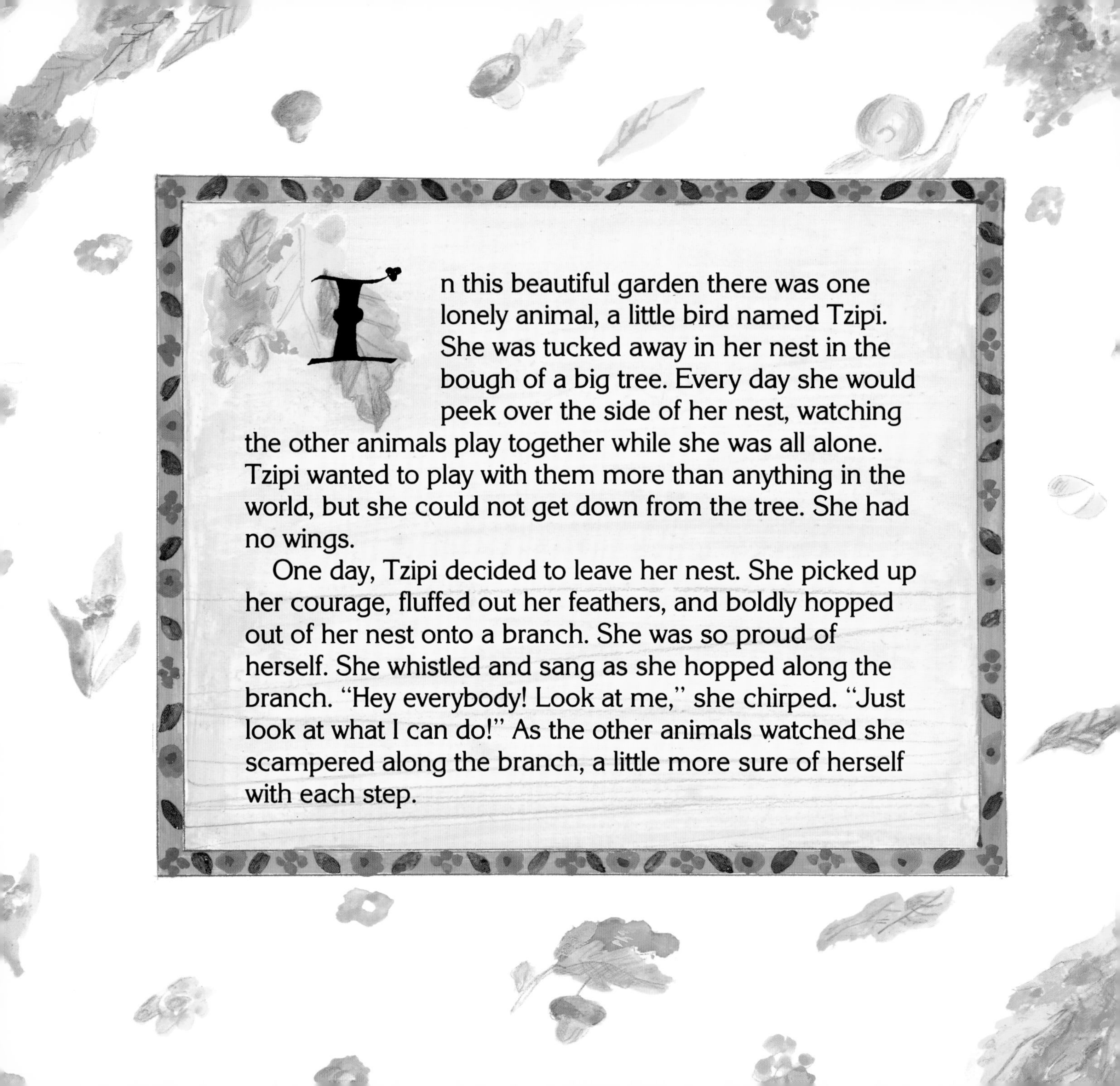

In this beautiful garden there was one lonely animal, a little bird named Tzipi. She was tucked away in her nest in the bough of a big tree. Every day she would peek over the side of her nest, watching the other animals play together while she was all alone. Tzipi wanted to play with them more than anything in the world, but she could not get down from the tree. She had no wings.

One day, Tzipi decided to leave her nest. She picked up her courage, fluffed out her feathers, and boldly hopped out of her nest onto a branch. She was so proud of herself. She whistled and sang as she hopped along the branch. "Hey everybody! Look at me," she chirped. "Just look at what I can do!" As the other animals watched she scampered along the branch, a little more sure of herself with each step.

That's pretty neat," barked the dog, wagging his tail. "Why don't you come down and play with us?"

"I can't," sighed the little bird. "It's too far for me to jump. Why don't you come up here to play?"

"Oh," whined the dog. "I'm sorry, but I can't climb trees. Besides, we like to play down here. It's more fun when we can all play together."

This made Tzipi very sad. In the morning she sat on the branch watching the other animals have fun in the beautiful garden, and wishing she could be with them. At night, she went to sleep alone in her nest, while the other animals slept peacefully beneath the trees.

Many days passed, and Tzipi kept wondering how she could come down from the tree so that she could play with all the other animals. As time went by, she saw that the animals were not playing together any more. Something was wrong in the garden.

The trees were drooping
the flowers were wilting
the hedges needed trimming
the grass needed mowing
and weeds were growing wild
everywhere.

God also saw that something was wrong. So God called all the animals together and said, "This was a beautiful garden, but it's not so beautiful any more. You haven't been taking care of it. The grass needs to be mowed and the bushes trimmed. The trees have to be pruned and the flowers must be watered. The stream needs to be cleaned, and the whole garden should be weeded. I gave you a wonderful garden. Your part was to keep the garden green and trim, neat and clean, so that you will have a good place in which to live and play."

The elephant said, "Oh God, don't worry! We'll clean up tomorrow!" But tomorrow came and went, and still the garden was not cleaned.

With each passing day, the garden looked worse and worse. The grass grew too high to roll in and the flowers began to droop their heads and turn brown. The bushes grew together, blocking the garden paths. God went to the animals one by one, asking for their help.

The lion roared, "I'm the king of the beasts. Kings do not clean!" And he stomped away, shaking his mane.

The cheetah said, "I'm too fast on my feet. I have no time to spend on grime!" She raced off into the tall grass.

The rhino snorted and stamped her feet. "If you won't clean up, I won't either!" She charged after the others.

The wolf howled, "How? I just don't know how!" She trotted back to her den with her head bent to the ground. The snake didn't say anything. He just quietly slithered away.

Each animal in turn refused to do its part, and God said, "Isn't there anyone who will help Me?" But silence fell upon the garden. No one spoke. No one even breathed. Then out of that silence came a tiny chirp. "I'll help You, God. Only I can't get down."

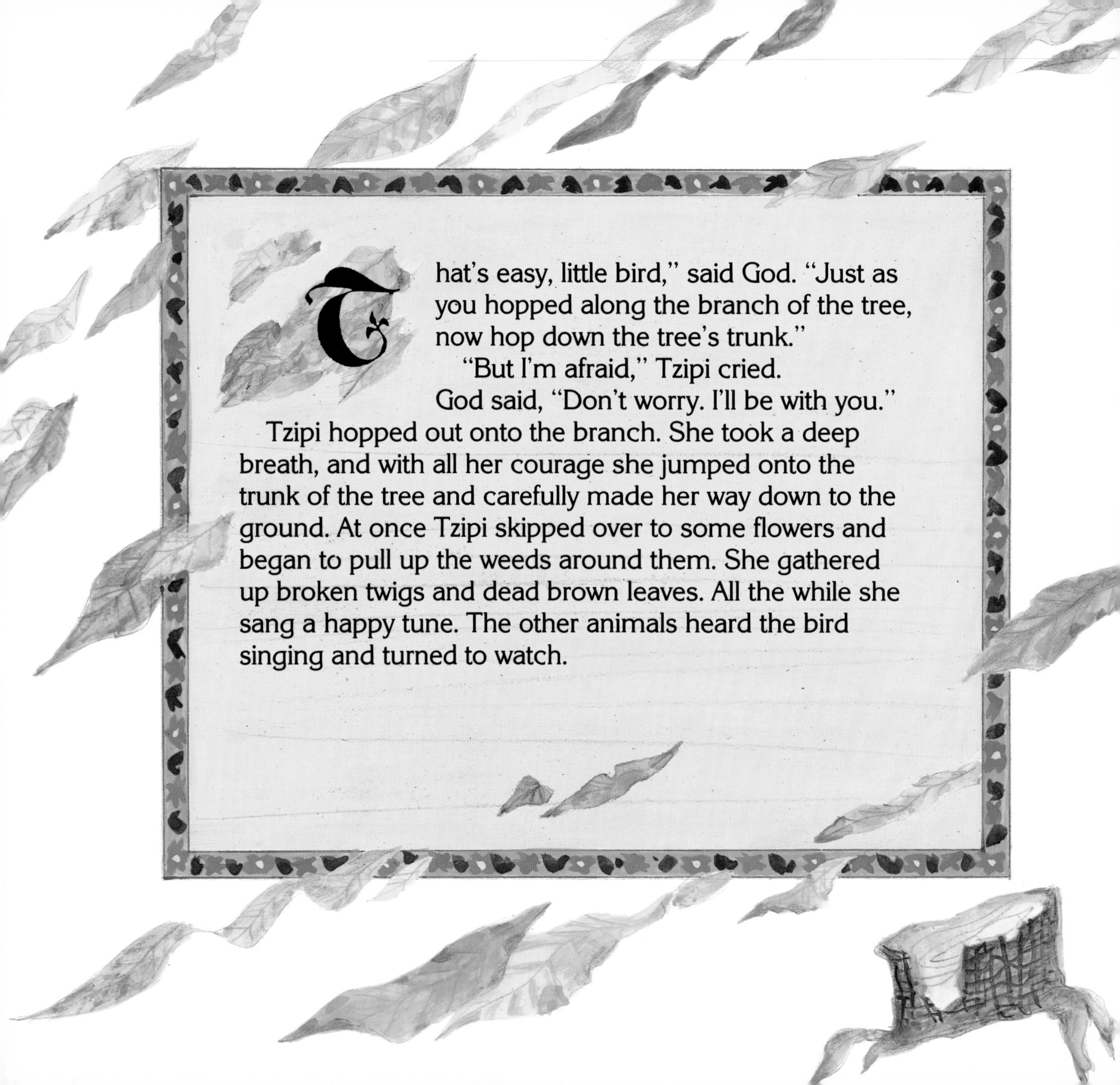

That's easy, little bird," said God. "Just as you hopped along the branch of the tree, now hop down the tree's trunk."

"But I'm afraid," Tzipi cried.

God said, "Don't worry. I'll be with you."

Tzipi hopped out onto the branch. She took a deep breath, and with all her courage she jumped onto the trunk of the tree and carefully made her way down to the ground. At once Tzipi skipped over to some flowers and began to pull up the weeds around them. She gathered up broken twigs and dead brown leaves. All the while she sang a happy tune. The other animals heard the bird singing and turned to watch.

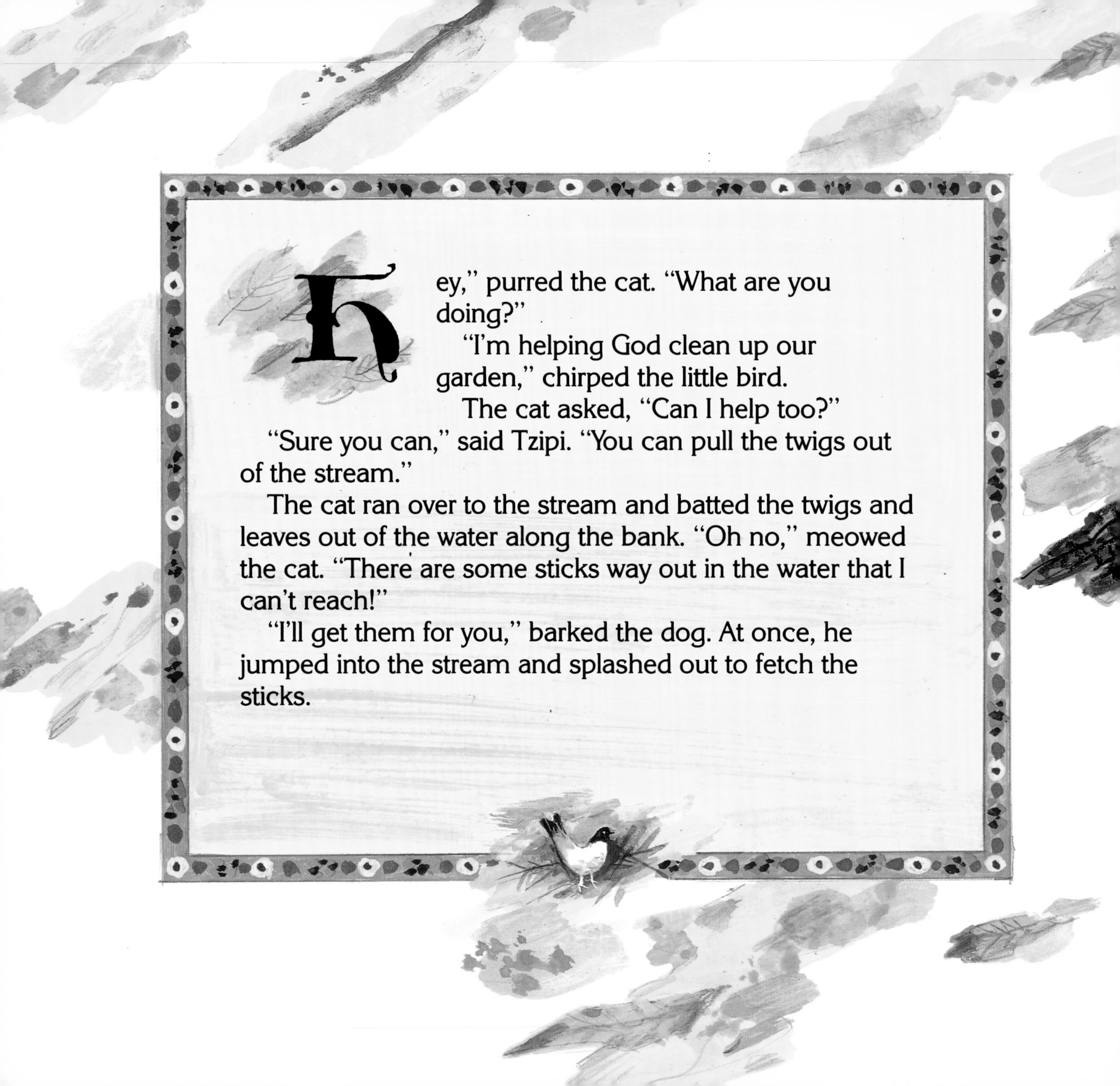

Hey," purred the cat. "What are you doing?"

"I'm helping God clean up our garden," chirped the little bird.

The cat asked, "Can I help too?"

"Sure you can," said Tzipi. "You can pull the twigs out of the stream."

The cat ran over to the stream and batted the twigs and leaves out of the water along the bank. "Oh no," meowed the cat. "There are some sticks way out in the water that I can't reach!"

"I'll get them for you," barked the dog. At once, he jumped into the stream and splashed out to fetch the sticks.

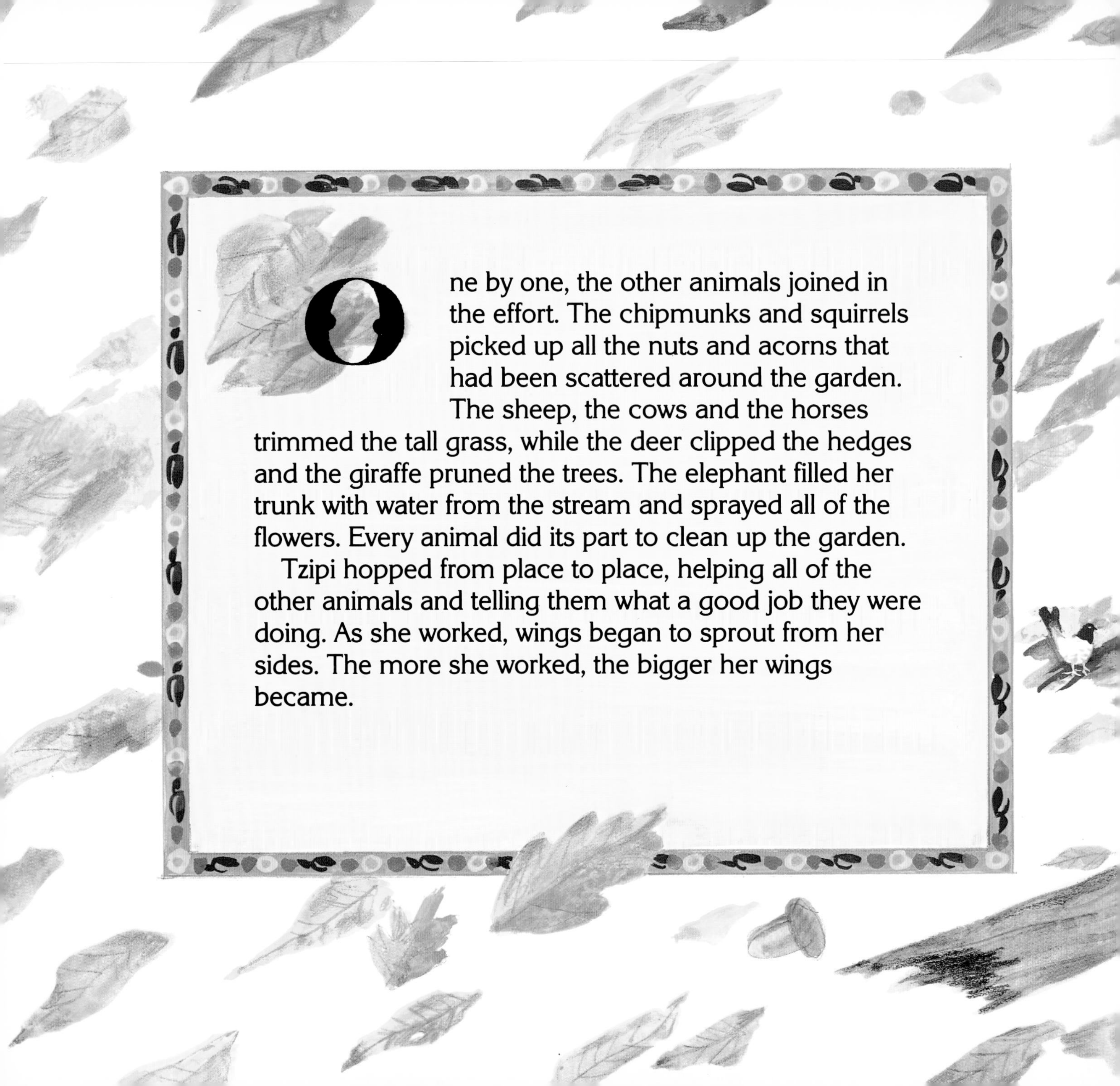

One by one, the other animals joined in the effort. The chipmunks and squirrels picked up all the nuts and acorns that had been scattered around the garden. The sheep, the cows and the horses trimmed the tall grass, while the deer clipped the hedges and the giraffe pruned the trees. The elephant filled her trunk with water from the stream and sprayed all of the flowers. Every animal did its part to clean up the garden.

Tzipi hopped from place to place, helping all of the other animals and telling them what a good job they were doing. As she worked, wings began to sprout from her sides. The more she worked, the bigger her wings became.

When the garden was completely clean, the little bird spread her wings and flew into the sky. As she glided from cloud to cloud and soared over the treetops, her happy song filled the garden.

And that's how Tzipi the bird got her wings.